ASHANTI
FESTIVAL

ASHANTI FESTIVAL

AND OTHER STORIES OF CHILDREN
AROUND THE WORLD
Compiled by the Editors
of
Highlights for Children

Compilation copyright © 1995 by Highlights for Children, Inc.
Contents copyright by Highlights for Children, Inc.
Published by Highlights for Children, Inc.
P.O. Box 18201
Columbus, Ohio 43218-0201
Printed in the United States of America

ISBN 0-87534-635-9

CONTENTS

Ashanti Festival by Lynda Pavlik 7

Su Ling's Secret by Pam Sandlin.......................13

Like an Antelope by Lee Ebler............................17

Maybe, a Maypole
by Elizabeth Van Steenwyk 23

Ti-Jean by Eleanor C. Wescott................................29

Pot Luck by David Lubar 35

On the Bog by Patrick L. Sullivan.........................41

Ming Potay and the Yeti Scream
by Sue Muller Hacking 45

Fiesta at San Isidro
by Nicolete Meredith Stack...51

Girma's Special Achievement
by Noel Habte-Mariam...57

Astradehojas Finds a Job
by Sophia Karageorges...63

Ntombi of Swaziland by James A. Jones 69

The Dragon's Bristle by D.J. Chaconas 73

A Gypsy Fortune by S. Jones Rogan 79

Pancho's Ferry by Bill Bollinger........................85

The Klompen Maker by Ann Lenssen 91

CONTENTS

ASHANTI FESTIVAL

By Lynda Pavlik

Kojo jumped out of bed with a big smile. His brown eyes sparkled with excitement. The day of the *durbar* had finally arrived.

Quickly, Kojo put on his *kente* cloth and new sandals. The warm African sun was just rising over the palm trees when Kojo ran outside.

"I don't have time to eat breakfast," Kojo told his mother. "Owusu and I are going to the *durbar*." His mother smiled as she put some *garri* into a bowl. "The *durbar* will not go away," she said.

"But we have to get there early," Kojo said anxiously. "Look. People are already going. We want to be in front to see the Ashanti King."

"You may go early," his mother assured him. "But you must also eat," she said as she gave Kojo his bowl of hot cereal.

Kojo sat down beside his mother. "Please tell me again about the *durbar*, Mother."

"A *durbar* is a very special festival for the Ashanti people," his mother explained. "There will be ceremonies and dancing. The drummers will play the talking drums. And there will be a lot of food—*fufu* and groundnut stew, *kenkey* and plaintain cakes."

Kojo filled his bowl again while he listened to his mother. "All the chiefs will come with their big umbrellas, the symbols of their authority," she continued. "Even the Ashanti King, the most important chief of all, will be there."

"I like the part about the food almost as much as the part about the King," Kojo said as he finished his second bowl of *garri*.

His mother laughed. "I'm sure you do. Your stomach is like a calabash," she said, "big and round on the outside and always empty on the inside."

Just then Kojo heard the throbbing of the drums begin. "I'm going to get Owusu now," Kojo said excitedly. "I'll see you at the *durbar*."

Kojo ran past a grove of banana trees and past the marketplace. He ran past some lizards sunning themselves. He ran past the schoolhouse. Finally he came to Owusu's house.

"Hi, Owusu. Are you ready to go?" Kojo called.

"I'm not going, Kojo," his friend replied. "Not now anyway."

Kojo couldn't believe what he heard. "Not going!" he cried. "But, Owusu! We've been planning this for months. If we don't go early, we won't get to see the King."

Owusu didn't say anything. He just sat there looking forlorn.

"What's the matter, Owusu?" Kojo asked gently as he sat down beside his friend. "Are you sick?"

"No, I'm not sick," Owusu replied sadly. "My mother is. I have to stay here to take care of my baby sister until my aunt comes," he explained quietly. "But you don't have to wait, Kojo. You go ahead," Owusu urged. "I'll come when I can."

Kojo walked slowly toward the *durbar*. Many people passed him. They were all going to the festival. Everyone was in a hurry.

Girls carrying trays of oranges and peanuts on their heads passed Kojo. Women with babies on their backs passed him. Even old men with walking sticks passed him.

Everyone was happy. Everyone except Kojo.

Kojo had nearly reached the place where the *durbar* was being held. He could hear the talking drums—*tum-pan, tum-pan*. He could see the big, bright umbrellas of the chiefs. He could smell the groundnut stew and the plaintain cakes. Perhaps if he hurried, he could still get near the King.

Then Kojo stopped. "But what about Owusu?" he thought. It only took Kojo a few seconds to make his decision.

He turned and ran back to Owusu's house.

"What are you doing here, Kojo?" Owusu was surprised when he saw his friend. "The *durbar* has already begun!"

"I know," Kojo answered cheerfully. "But it won't go away. Besides, I thought you might like to have some company while you wait for your aunt."

Kojo and Owusu sat playing with Owusu's baby sister in the shade of a mango tree. The sun was getting hotter, and the road was soon crowded with festival-goers.

It wasn't long before four of their friends passed by. "What are you two doing?" one of them asked. "I thought you were going to be the first ones at the *durbar!*" The friends snickered.

"We changed our plans," Kojo answered calmly as he continued playing with the baby.

"You're missing all the excitement," another boy said. "The King lost his gold ring, and all of us are helping to look for it," he boasted. "You could come with us."

More than anything, Kojo wanted to go. He looked at Owusu and knew that he did, too. Neither of them said anything for a few minutes.

"No," Kojo said as he stood up and adjusted his *kente* cloth over his shoulder. "No, we'll come later."

It was a long time after the four friends had run off, leaving Kojo and Owusu alone, that Owusu's aunt arrived. The sun was already high in the sky, and the road to the *durbar* was deserted.

Kojo and Owusu ran down the empty road as fast as they could. In the distance they could hear the steady beat of the drums.

Suddenly, a tiny glitter in the dust caught Kojo's eye. Kojo yelled excitedly as he bent over the shiny object. "Look what I found! It's the ring that the King lost!" he cried.

With Kojo gripping the golden ring tightly in his fist, the two boys sped down the road. The throbbing of the drums grew louder and louder. The crowd grew thicker and thicker.

The ring still clutched in his hand, Kojo looked around the dense crowd. He knew they would never get through to the King.

Then Kojo saw one of the King's horn blowers. Squirming through the tightly packed bodies, Kojo and Owusu finally reached the tall, dignified man.

"Excuse me, sir," Kojo said loudly in order to be heard over the noise of the crowd. "We found the King's ring on the road," he explained. "Would you please give it to him?" Kojo asked politely.

The tall man looked down at the two young boys, dusty and hot from running. "No, I won't," the horn blower declared, as a slow smile spread across his face. "I won't give it to him," the horn blower continued, "but you can!"

Blowing his horn of ivory, the horn blower cleared a path to the King for Kojo and Owusu.

The great Ashanti King sat on his throne under an enormous red umbrella. He was surrounded by attendants and dazzling gold ornaments. Kojo and Owusu were speechless with awe.

When Kojo timidly gave the King his golden ring, the Ashanti King said kindly, "You are a good Ashanti boy. Come, I want you and your friend to sit near me for the ceremonies today."

The mighty drums talked. The dancers leaped and whirled.

And Kojo ate. He ate more than he had ever eaten before.

It was a *durbar* Kojo would never forget.

Su Ling's Secret

By Pam Sandlin

Su Ling was playing quietly in the garden when a rustling noise caught her attention. She hardly dared to breathe as she kept her eyes on the yew tree from which the sound had seemed to come. As she watched, the lower branches of the tree shook gently. Su Ling's almond eyes grew wide in astonishment as a *dragon* emerged into the sunlight. Green scales glistened as though sprinkled with diamond dust.

It raised its scaly head and looked to the left and to the right. Su Ling held perfectly still, hoping it would not notice her there. The dragon turned sharply, and its long tail grazed a nearby cedar tree, causing it to tremble. With a long red tongue, the dragon investigated the roof of the pagoda, which was set in the middle of the garden. Finding it to his liking, he clambered onto the roof and proceeded to bask in the warmth of the sun.

Su Ling watched the drowsy dragon for a long time. Finally, when she was sure he had gone to sleep, she inched backward until she could no longer see the pagoda. She ran to the house. Before she could tell her exciting news, her mother informed her that dinner was ready, right now. Hurriedly, Su Ling washed her face and hands and joined them at the table. As they ate, her father and mother discussed their day. Su Ling said nothing, for she was daydreaming about the dragon. As her mother went to get dessert, Su Ling's father turned to her.

"How was your day, Su Ling?" he asked.

"Just wonderful, Father," she replied. "I have been by the garden all afternoon."

Su Ling smiled as she thought of the garden and her very own dragon there.

"My daughter," her father said, "You have the look of one with a secret. Is this a secret you may share?"

"Yes, my father," she giggled. "Do you know that we have a dragon in the garden?"

Her father's eyebrows raised so high that Su Ling could not help laughing.

"A dragon!" he exclaimed. "You would not tell me an untruth, would you, Little One?"

"Oh, no," she protested. "There really *is* a dragon!"

"Might one so grown up as myself be permitted to look upon this wonder?" her father asked, his eyes twinkling.

"Yes, Father, if he has not gone away," she said.

After their meal was over, Su Ling and her father went outside and walked to the garden.

"Where was this dragon, my daughter?"

"He was sleeping on the roof of the pagoda when I left, Father," Su Ling whispered.

They moved silently until they could see the small temple.

Su Ling smiled with delight. Her dragon was still there, sleeping. Her father took a long look. Then he chuckled aloud and woke the dragon! In a flash it leaped from the pagoda, knocking it over, and scurried away.

"You frightened him," Su Ling accused. "He is only a baby and still shy!"

Her father laughed again and sat down on a low bench by the pagoda. With one hand, he set the small replica back on its base among the miniature bonsai trees in the rock garden.

"Are you *sure* it was a dragon, Su Ling?" her parent questioned. "Or could it have been only a small lizard, sunning himself on the tiny pagoda in our modest rock garden?"

Su Ling thought for a moment. Then she sighed with disappointment.

"I had *hoped* it was a baby dragon! You know, there are not many dragons around anymore," she murmured. "I suppose it really was a lizard, though."

"It may be a good thing, Little One, that it was not a dragon," her father said very seriously. "Do you wonder why?"

When she nodded, he continued.

"If, indeed, we did have a baby dragon in the garden," he asked, "where would we put his large, full-grown parents?"

Su Ling put both hands to her lips to quiet the laughter that came rolling out. She had not considered BIG dragons at all!

"Perhaps you are right, my father," she giggled. "We have room for only a bonsai dragon!"

LIKE AN ANTELOPE

By Lee Ebler

Tata stood very still with his arm about Small One. He had to stand quietly or Small One would fall. Small One was one of five Indian children born crippled during the Winter of Sickness. Tata had been born that same year, but he had been fortunate. He walked with only a small limp.

"Look!" said Small One, almost dropping his stick-crutch in his excitement. "Here they come!"

The Sioux children were racing. They were running on the path that went around the village of buffalo-skin tipis. They laughed as the dust rolled behind them, but they also worked. Old Chief expected them to run. The running would turn them into swift, strong warriors.

"Old Chief has stopped his carving to watch," said Tata. "My mother says he finds the next tribal leaders in the races."

"Oh, Red Bow has stumbled!" said Small One, trying to see around the little crowd that had joined them.

"And you will fall, too, if you don't hold still," said Tata, tightening his grip on his friend.

"You should race, Tata," said Small One suddenly. "You are old enough now."

"I will never be a good runner," said Tata. "My legs are not fast. I would come in last and look foolish. It is better that I stay with you."

"You move well," said Small One loyally. "You are strong, and I can walk when I'm with you."

"Sometimes I want to run," admitted Tata. "Sometimes I'm sad that I limp."

"I am sad in my heart, too," said Small One, and hung his head.

Tata was sorry for his words. He had much freedom, while Small One spent most of his time in the shade of his tipi, helping his mother pound berries and buffalo meat into *pemmican*.

"Small One?"

But Small One would not answer.

"Small One, talk to me! When you are unhappy, you get as still as the snake that plays dead."

"I would like to run like an antelope," said Small One. "I would like to taste the wind."

Tata watched the runners disappear behind Wolf Rock. If he and Small One joined the race, they would come in last. Their eyes and noses would be filled with the dust of those who were quicker. Others might laugh at them.

But Small One wanted to run like an antelope.

"Let's run," said Tata. "They will let us. We will not run fast, but we will be in the race."

"We could not run at all," said Small One. "We could only walk."

"Even an antelope walks before it runs," said Tata. "Come, Small One. It will be an adventure, and I will help you."

Small One smiled. "All right. We will . . . walk like an antelope."

As they made their way through the crowd, some of the children whispered. But Tata's thoughts were on Small One. When Small One reached the dirt path, he put part of his weight on the stick-crutch and part on Tata's arm. They started off at an uneven pace.

"We are bumping like a three-legged horse!" said Small One. "We will give each other blisters!"

"Put your stick down as I put down my right foot," said Tata. "There is a rhythm to walking as there is a rhythm to the moon and sun."

"Sometimes you cannot see the moon and sun," said Small One, panting.

"Old Chief says the moon and sun are always there," said Tata, and just then they found their rhythm. It was not fast, but it was smooth.

"Step together!" said Tata, catching his breath. "Together. Faster now!"

They were walking. The other runners were far ahead. The dust was gone, and the world was warm and bright. Without looking, Tata knew they were passing the cooking pits. He could smell the woodsmoke. And he could hear . . . hear the quiet. The runners were not laughing now, and the crowd was not cheering. But Tata was too busy to wonder. It was hard work walking Small One.

They got to the end of the village where Wolf Rock stood. Tata thought his arm would break, but he could not let go of Small One.

"We are almost back," he said. "How are you, Small One?"

"Like a hunted antelope, Tata, but I am tasting the wind."

Finally they puffed their way back to where the other runners stood waiting, and Old Chief was there, too. It was then that Tata thought about the quiet. It was a waiting kind of quiet.

"Are we in trouble?" whispered Small One.

Tata did not know.

"Good race," said Old Chief in his deep voice. "Good race to Quick Shadow who ran fastest. Good race to Red Bow, who fell and got up to run again." Then he looked at Small One and Tata. "Good race to Small One, who cannot run, but did. Good race to Tata, who has become strong by helping his friend. Warriors are made from such love and work." Then he turned and went slowly back to his tipi.

"He said we ran," said Small One happily.

Tata nodded. "In our hearts," he said, "we ran like antelopes."

Maybe, a Maypole

By Elizabeth Van Steenwyk

Meeka stood before the class, trying to find the right words to recite her lessons. She felt so tall and skinny in her old clothes from Sweden. And she sounded funny, too. Now, when she heard her classmates laughing as she tried to speak English, she knew her face burned the same color as her bright orange-red hair. She wouldn't cry though. Eleven-year-olds do not cry, especially in front of little first-graders.

"Thank you, Meeka," Miss Dean said. "You may be seated."

Meeka ran to her seat, threw herself down, and grabbed her lesson book. She opened it and buried her face inside, then stared at the date on her spelling word list. *April 25, 1913.* Oh, why did her family have to leave Sweden two months ago? But she knew why—because there'd been no work for Papa. They came to America so he could work and they could live better. But she'd never feel at home here. Not in this country, not even in this room.

Soon Miss Dean rang the bell for recess, and everyone scrambled outside. Everyone but Meeka. Recess was as hard as reciting.

"Meeka, aren't you going out?" Miss Dean asked.

Meeka stood up and walked slowly to the door. "I don't belong here, Miss Dean. I shouldn't be with the first-graders."

"As soon as you learn to speak English better, you will be placed in sixth grade with children your own age," Miss Dean said. "But you need to talk more so your skill will improve. Won't you try harder?"

"*Ja,*" Meeka said, then smiled. "I mean, yes."

"It's nice to see you smile," Miss Dean answered.

Meeka walked to the playground and watched as everyone played stickball or jumped rope. At home in Sweden it would be somewhat the same, except that by now they'd be working on their maypole dances, too. In her mind she danced through the Three Karls Polka, one of her favorites. This way, then that way, in and out.

"Are you dancing?" someone asked.

Meeka looked down into the face of JoBess, one of her classmates.

"No," she said, feeling foolish again.

"Yes, you were," JoBess insisted. "Will you show me how?"

"If you promise not to laugh." Then Meeka hummed and danced through the Ox Trot, pleased that JoBess learned so quickly.

Back in the classroom, JoBess raised her hand. "Meeka knows how to dance and sing."

Miss Dean looked interested. "Would you show the rest of us, Meeka?"

At first she felt clumsy, but once Meeka began, she forgot everything else and thought only of the maypole dance. When she finished, everyone clapped.

"Maybe you'd like to explain the maypole tradition in Sweden," Miss Dean said.

Meeka took a deep breath and began, hoping she wouldn't make too many mistakes. She told them that each year on the Saturday nearest June 24, the day of midsummer, the men chop down a tall, thin birch tree, then set it up in the village square. It is called a maypole, not because of the month, but because of the Swedish word *maj*, which refers to decorating with greens and flowers.

And that's what everyone does, Meeka went on. Everyone, boys and girls especially, decorates the long pole with garlands of birch leaves and wild-flowers. Then dancers join hands, circling the may-pole, weaving in and out while a fiddler plays the Three Karls Polka, the Ox Trot, and the Windmill Dance. Feasting and dancing continue until morn-ing, as everyone celebrates the longest day of the year in Sweden. The day when the sun never sets.

When Meeka finished, the classroom was com-pletely silent. She felt uneasy—had they not understood her funny English?

Finally Clara spoke. "I wish we could have a maypole here this year."

"It's up to Meeka," Miss Dean said. "Will you show us how?"

Meeka felt her heart skip nervously. "*Ja*, I'll try," she answered. The songs, the dancing, the decora-tions were easy. But how would she get a may-pole? How could she chop down a tree?

The next morning at recess she began to teach the dancing. She sang the old songs in a clear, bright voice and soon the other children were humming along, even trying to sing some of the Swedish words.

"I think the other students in school should see you dance," Miss Dean said. "Will you be ready next Monday?"

"*Ja,*" Meeka replied. She felt she could do it, except . . . except . . .

During afternoon recesses, Meeka led her class-mates to the nearby woods, where they gathered early blooms and bright leaves. Then she showed how to sew them on long strands of twine. By week's end, they had baskets heaped with long garlands. They'd be ready on Monday. Maybe.

She was very worried as she walked home on Friday afternoon. The next day she worried even more. She tried to ask Papa for his help when he came home from work, but he was too tired to talk.

Meeka walked slowly home from church the next afternoon, finding little comfort in the late sun. What was she going to do? Where could she find a maypole? Then she stopped. Her long shadow stopped beside her. Oh, *ja.* Would it work? She had to try. Maybe that was the answer.

Meeka dressed in her finest clothes and hurried to school early the next morning.

"Are you ready?" Miss Dean asked.

"*Ja,*" Meeka said.

At noon all the children in school gathered on the playground. Miss Dean hurried up, looking worried. "Where is the maypole?" she asked.

"Watch," Meeka said, smiling. Quickly she picked up the garlands, then wound them around her waist and arms and shoulders. Next she tucked some flowers in her hair. Then she walked to the center of the playground where everyone was waiting. Her small classmates followed.

"Now," she whispered. "Now sing and dance around me."

And they did. They joined hands and circled her, then danced in the warm sunshine without missing a step, as they sang the Swedish songs that Meeka had taught them. When they finished, everyone clapped and asked for more.

"Am I your favorite maypole?" she whispered to them as they began again.

"*Ja,*" they answered. No one laughed harder than Meeka. And no one felt more at home.

TI-JEAN

By Eleanor C. Wescott

Ti-Jean's name means "Little John" in the Creole district of his native island of Haiti.

One summer day he stood in the doorway of his one-room, thatched cottage on a hillside that rose above the white capital city. Behind him stretched purple mountains from which came the sound of drumbeats every night. Flowers nodded, birds called, and palm branches waved, but Ti-Jean was sad. His mother and two small sisters were hungry.

"How can I buy a goat," he wondered, "so we can drink milk every day?" Then he had an idea.

Chewing a stalk of sugarcane, he climbed to the pink house where his aunt worked for an artist and his wife. They were packing to leave for the mountains, for it was very hot near the city. Ti-Jean told Tante Bertha his plan. She nodded. Then she went to the artist and his wife and said, "Monsieur, Madame, my nephew Ti-Jean wants to go with us and work as your houseboy."

So that afternoon Ti-Jean said good-bye to his family and got into the car waiting to take him to the mountains. It was his first automobile ride, up a long road winding between poinsettia and red bougainvillaea bushes. The evening air was cool when they reached the big house with the pointed roof and deep porches. Ti-Jean's eyes, round with wonder, were like white saucers in the dark. That night, instead of a straw mat on the floor, he slept in a bed for the first time in his life.

Early next morning he saw women walking down the dusty road with baskets on their heads— baskets filled with yellow mangoes, bright red tomatoes, and green avocados. He followed them to the noisy, cluttered marketplace in the nearby village, where shoes, mahogany tables, chickens, and everything else imaginable was for sale.

Then, in front of an open-air booth, he saw the goat he wanted to take home to his family. He fell on his knees beside the goat, stroking her silvery hair. She pawed the ground with her cloven hoofs. Right then he named her *Ou-Belle,* which in Creole means "You're beautiful."

But Mère Marie, behind the wooden counter, called, "Go away, little boy! My goat is for sale. We need money."

Ti-Jean nodded. "I will buy her soon," he promised. "I am working."

Each day he helped Tante Bertha. He swept the floors, weeded the garden, and served meals to Monsieur and Madame. He made coffee for Monsieur, who painted scenes of Haiti in the gold of the day and with the green flashes at sunset. In the evenings, Ti-Jean brought home his new friend, Grand-Armand, who played a drum made from a hollowed tree. The rhythm of this tambour drum is like a second language in Haiti.

Every morning Ti-Jean followed the women to market, and each day his heart seemed to jump from his toes to his mouth until he saw that Ou-Belle was still there. She would nuzzle him, munching the grass he brought her. But Mère Marie was very poor, and always she repeated, "My goat is for sale."

31

Through the weeks Monsieur and Madame thought Ti-Jean was happy, until one night they heard a sound like the wind sighing through the breadfruit trees. Ti-Jean was crying. In the morning they spoke to Tante Bertha.

"He dreamed that his family was hungry," she said. "All summer he has been saving to buy a milk goat at the market, but there is not yet enough money, and every day he is afraid that someone else will buy her."

Monsieur called Ti-Jean over to where he was sitting. "Now you have earned enough money," he said, handing Ti-Jean 200 gourdes. "Would you like to buy the goat and take her home today?"

Ti-Jean's bare feet stirred clouds of dust as he raced down the road. But what was that moving away? It was a tall man, pulling Ou-Belle by a rope. Ti-Jean started after them, but he stumbled and fell. "Ou-Belle!" he screamed.

The goat turned. With a heave, she broke away and galloped to the boy. Together they stood in the white road on which the man's huge shadow was reflected. Mère Marie's shadow was there, too, shaking a spindly finger. The air was filled with their shouting voices. Ti-Jean's money was scattered in the dust. Then they looked at the small boy crouching beside the goat, his arms around her neck, while tears made little rivers down his dusty cheeks.

Suddenly the man's scowl turned into a flashing smile. "I will take another goat," he said. "This one belongs with the boy."

Ti-Jean scrambled after his money, and his hands shook as he paid for Ou-Belle. Then he led her, now his own goat, back to the big house.

Later that day, while Grand-Armand beat a farewell on the tambour, Tante Bertha, Monsieur, Madame, and Mère Marie waved good-bye as Ti-Jean and Ou-Belle boarded a large, green, open bus called a "tap-tap." On the side in red letters was painted its name, *Venez avec Moi* (Come with Me). The passengers pushed each other on the wooden benches and sang as the bus rattled down the mountainside. Ou-Belle nibbled the driver's collar, but he only laughed. And when they reached the hillside where Ti-Jean lived, the driver gently lifted them down.

Ti-Jean's small sisters skipped toward Ti-Jean and the goat. Doors opened, and the neighbors came out, admiring the goat who lifted her head with pride. Then they lined the pathway, making an aisle for the little girls, followed by their brother, the manly boy who had earned the money so that his family would always have milk to drink and would never be hungry again. Down the path Ti-Jean marched, holding Ou-Belle's rope, until he reached his mother and placed the rope in her waiting hands.

Everyone was smiling, and the Haitian sun, always beaming, seemed to shine just a little brighter than ever before.

Pot Luck

By David Lubar

Teresa knew something good was going on when she walked into the kitchen. A big pot was bubbling on the stove, sending the wonderful aroma of tomatoes and oregano through the air. At the counter, Mrs. Rosario was kneading dough.

"What are you making, Mom?" Teresa asked.

"*Tortellini,*" her mother answered.

"Great." This was a real treat. Teresa loved the way her mother made little pockets of noodles stuffed with seasoned meat. The *tortellini,* like small *ravioli,* were covered with her mom's spectacular sauce. It was heaven in a bowl.

"We've been invited to a pot-luck dinner to meet some of our neighbors tonight."

"Pot luck?" Teresa asked.

"Everyone brings a different dish to eat and we all share. It'll be fun. Now go play and try to meet some more friends."

Teresa ran outside. So far, she liked her new home. It was very different from her old home. Almost everyone in the old neighborhood was Italian. Nobody else in the new neighborhood was Italian. But the kids she'd met were nice, even if they were different. She'd already made a few friends. There was a playground behind the row of houses. She saw Esther Goldenberg and Kay Yamamoto playing on the swings.

"Are you going to the dinner tonight?" Kay asked when Teresa reached the girls.

"Yup, my mom's making her super-duper *tortellini.*"

Kay seemed to look a bit puzzled. Then she smiled and said, "I can't wait. My dad is making *gyozo.* And I heard that Kami Shen's mom is making *shao mai.*"

Gyozo, Teresa thought. She didn't have any idea what that was, though she suspected it was a

Japanese food since Kay's parents came from Japan. She hadn't heard of *shao mai* either. Kami's grandparents had come from China. Teresa couldn't admit that she didn't know what those things were. Maybe I can ask Esther, she thought. Later, when Kay was called in for lunch, Teresa had her chance.

"What is *gyozo?*" she asked Esther.

Esther shook her head. "I was hoping you would know. I hope it isn't something icky."

"Why would it be?" Teresa asked.

"People eat all kinds of things. You know, they eat whale fat in Alaska. I heard that some people eat ants. Who knows what that stuff is."

"Do you think we'll have to eat it tonight?"

"I don't think we have a choice," Esther told her. "It's rude not to try everything at a pot-luck dinner. At least you'll be safe with what we're bringing. My mom is making *kreplach*." She jumped from the swing and ran off, saying she wanted to watch her mom cook.

Teresa just sat there. She had never heard of *kreplach* either. Esther's ancestors came from Russia and Poland and were Jewish. Russia wasn't all that far from Italy. How could their food be so different? This might not be much fun, Teresa thought. She didn't know what she would do if something really awful was on her plate. But these were her friends; they couldn't eat anything that strange, could they? At least there would be *tortellini*. Everyone loves *tortellini*. Teresa went back in to see if she could help her mom.

That evening, Teresa went with her parents to the house next door. Mr. Shen greeted them with a big smile. "Come on in," he said, taking the pot from Mrs. Rosario. "Welcome to our house, and to the neighborhood. This smells wonderful." Teresa walked over to join the rest of the children. Before she knew it, it was time to eat. She went up to a big table in the dining room, walking between Esther and Kay. She promised herself that she would try her best to eat the food, no matter how terrible it might be.

"I hope I like everything," she said quietly.

"I'm sure it's all great," Kay said. "Though I have a confession to make."

"What?" Teresa asked her.

"I was afraid to say, but I don't know what *tortellini* is. It isn't anything yucky, is it, like with snails or something?"

Teresa laughed at the thought. "It's just a noodle stuffed with meat. But what is . . ." she couldn't remember the name.

"*Gyozo?*" Kay asked. She pointed to the table.

"It's a noodle stuffed with meat. Actually, you could say the same about *shao mai*."

Teresa looked at the table. She took a small helping of each thing. "And this?" she asked, pointing to another type of noodle.

"That's *kreplach*," Esther said. "It's a noodle stuffed with meat."

"We have something just like that, but we call it a *won ton*," Kami Shen said as she joined the group. "Well, it all looks great. What's that?" she asked, pointing to a bowl with white noodles in red sauce.

"That's *tortellini*," Teresa said. "It's a noodle filled with meat." Teresa laughed at the words. She took a bite of *gyozo*. It was delicious. Then she tried the *shao mai* and the *kreplach*. "Everything is wonderful," she said. "It's all sort of the same, but each thing is different in a special way." She looked around at the kids in the room. Just like us, she thought, the same, but different in special and wonderful ways. Then, because the thought was just too good to keep to herself, she repeated it to her new friends.

On the Bog

By Patrick L. Sullivan

Ireland is a small country across the Atlantic Ocean from the United States. We have lived in Ireland for two years and like it very much. At least, we like it most of the time. Last winter, though, oil to heat the house became very expensive and hard to get. We had some very cold days, and Dad would say to Mom, "Bridget, if the oil bills get any higher, we will have to sell the house to pay them." Or he would say, "Bridget, can't we turn the thermostat down a few more degrees?"

And finally he said to me, "Tommy, if we don't freeze before then, in the spring you and I are going to cut turf for next winter."

I wasn't sure what he meant, but Dad is always saying things that a kid can't understand. Then, spring did come, and one Friday night Dad sent me to bed early. "Tomorrow we are going to cut turf." He got me up very early the next morning.

We drove out of the city and a long way into the country. While he drove, Dad told me how he had written to the County Council and rented a *rod* of turf bog. A *rod* is a piece of ground about sixteen feet on a side. On our *rod* we could dig all the turf we could get. Then he tried to explain how the turf looked like dirt sods and burned like coal, and how it was decayed vegetation from thousands of years ago. I fell asleep, though, because it was really early in the morning.

I had thought that a bog would be a marsh, half-underwater with frogs and snakes. Instead, it looked just like normal ground except it was springy to walk on and the soil was very dark. It was a sunny day. Groups of men were digging in several places already. Dad parked by the side of the road and we got out of the car with our tools.

Dad had a map, but he couldn't find our *rod*. He asked one of the men, who showed us where we were to dig. An old man and his sons said that they had come to this bog to cut turf for many years. On their farm, they used turf not only for heat but also for cooking. The old man sent his sons back to work, and he stayed to help Dad. He set himself down on a moss-grown dirt pile near our *rod* and began to tell Dad what to do. Dad was clearing the dirt and grass off the top of the turf when the old man stopped him. The best turf was deeper, and a beginner would never be able to go deep enough over a whole rod in one day. It was better to have a deep, narrow hole than a shallow, wide one.

Dad took the *slane* then. The *slane* is like a long-handled spade, but the blade is L-shaped instead of flat. Dad was supposed to use the *slane* to cut long, narrow pieces of turf out of the bog. Dad wasn't very good at first, but soon he was cutting neat, square pieces of turf.

Turf is cut one layer at a time. Each layer is about eight inches. The old man called each layer a *spit*. On this bog, he said, a good cutter could get eleven *spits* before water seeped into the hole.

While Dad was cutting out pieces of turf, the old man showed me how to gather them in the wheelbarrow we had brought. I wheeled them out from Dad's hole and lined them up on the bog so the sun would dry them. It was hard work. When lunchtime came I was happy to stop.

After lunch, Dad went back to cutting turf, I kept spreading it out to dry, and the old man watched and smoked his pipe. As Dad was just starting his seventh *spit,* water began seeping into the bottom of our hole. The old man walked over, looked into the hole, and said that that was all the turf we would cut out of that hole.

We didn't bring the turf back with us that day. We came back to the bog in a few weeks and turned over all the pieces I had laid out so that the sun could dry the other side. Then, after a few more weeks, we went out again and stacked them in little piles called *foots.* Finally, in the fall, we rented a trailer for the car and collected all the turf. At home we put it in the shed.

Now that it's winter again, Dad will send me out for a bucket of turf for the fire. Then we can sit in the living room and be warmed by the turf that we cut out of the ground. It is a nice feeling to see that fire.

Dad still complains about the price of oil, but I tell him that we will go out and get more turf in the spring. He smiles and says that he hopes we can. I hope so, too.

MING POTAY
AND THE YETI
SCREAM

By Sue Muller Hacking

Ming Potay woke up when the tent flap brushed her face. A cold wind from the Himalayan glaciers stung her nose.

A long, drawn-out moan and a high-pitched whistle cut the night air. *Ohooon-Tzeeee!*

"Mother," whispered Ming Potay. "Did you hear that? It makes my neck prickle."

"It's the bushes groaning in the wind," said her mother. "Go back to sleep."

The bushes? she thought. Just the bushes. She lay still a long time before falling asleep.

Clanging pots, laughter, and singing lured Ming Potay from her tent in the early dawn. Long blue shadows lay over the meadow by the monastery.

"Ming Potay!" called her mother. "Eat now. We have work to do."

Ming Potay dipped a cold potato in salt, then swallowed it in two bites. She sipped warm Tibetan tea, seasoned with butter and salt.

The Sherpa women sat near the fire to drink tea, scrub pots, and talk. Some men carried burned timbers from the monastery. Others started on the long trek to the village to collect pipes and sheet roofing. Everyone had a job to do, rebuilding the monastery. Ming Potay and her cousin, Nima Yangji, were sent to the river for water.

"Did you hear the yeti scream again last night?" Nima Yangji asked as they walked down the steep path toward the river.

Startled, Ming Potay replied, "Our teacher says the yeti is just a myth."

"But I've heard it," Nima Yangji said. "It moans and it screams in the night."

Ming Potay shivered. She too had heard the strange sounds. She remembered the stories that her grandmother told of the hairy manlike creatures living in caves, stealing yaks and sometimes people to eat.

"I don't believe in yetis, but something is making that sound," Ming Potay said. "Tonight we will find out what it is."

Nima Yangji nodded, but she looked scared.

At the river the cousins filled their jugs with icy water, then hefted the jugs to their backs. They trudged up the trail to the monastery.

After two trips up and down the trail, the cousins stopped for lunch beside the rushing river. Nearby, an old Sherpa man sat on a rock and played haunting tunes on his flute. After a while he let Ming Potay try to play. She laughed at the thin, airy sounds she made.

"Come, Ming Potay, we have work to do," Nima Yangji said with a laugh.

They made two more trips before the setting sun bathed the mountains in crimson light. Ming Potay and Nima Yangji retired early to their tents, and fell asleep to the sounds of adults singing.

The moon cast a silver light on the meadow. Ming Potay crawled out of her tent and shook Nima Yangji awake. The cousins picked their way around the dark mounds of sleeping yaks.

The wind had settled to a gentle breeze, and it was not quite as cold as the night before.

"Let's sit here," Nima Yangji said as they approached a pile of construction materials. The girls sat with their backs to the pipes and faced the wind.

They waited. They listened. Yak bells clanged and the bushes shook. But no screams cut the night. The wind blew harder, and they shivered.

"We must go back," Ming Potay said. "Now we'll never know what was making that sound."

"I'm glad we didn't hear it," said Nima Yangji as they retraced their route over the meadow.

Ohooon-Tzeeee!

Ming Potay grabbed her cousin's arm and pulled her to the ground beside a sleeping yak. The animal stirred and grunted, then slept.

Ohooon-Tzeeee!

I don't believe in yetis, thought Ming Potay. I really don't.

She peeked over the yak and saw the piles of pipe and roofing, and felt the wind in her face. The moan and the whistle came again.

Suddenly Ming Potay remembered the flute, and she giggled. Pulling her cousin from behind the yak, she said, "Come on, Nima Yangji. I'll show you the yeti."

They walked toward the pile of pipes. "Stay here and listen," she told Nima Yangji. "I'll make the yeti be quiet." She walked to the far side of the pile.

A strong breeze billowed her dress. "Do you hear it now?"

"Yes," called Nima Yangji.

Ming Potay moved between the wind and the open ends of the pipes.

"It stopped," said Nima Yangji, surprised.

"Our yeti is the wind," said Ming Potay. "And he plays the pipes better than I play the flute."

The two girls laughed. They linked arms and threaded their way through the meadow full of yaks, back to their tents.

Fiesta at San Isidro

By Nicolete Meredith Stack

Juan Panay jumped to his feet as the first rays of the warm Philippine sun came through the shell window of his nipa-thatched home. He rolled up his sleeping mat and went into the kitchen, where his mother was boiling rice in a big pot for his breakfast.

"Today is the day I've been waiting for, Nanay," he said. "I know that my onions will win first prize at the fiesta."

"I hope that is true, Juan," answered his mother. "You have worked so hard growing the onions, and they are very beautiful."

She looked at the bamboo basket. The basket was lined with green banana leaves on which the shiny pink Bermuda onions were arranged.

"That prize—three pesos! We could use that in this house, couldn't we, Nanay?"

Juan's mother did not answer. Even with her small income, she planned to put aside the prize money for Juan's education if he won.

"I must start soon," said Juan. "I think there will not be many onions as beautiful as mine."

"There will not be *any* onions like yours," answered his mother, "not here on the farms on Manila Bay."

"Next year there will be onions, though, Nanay. Padre Ignacio is going to distribute the seed I gave him to the farmers. He said he never has seen so fine an onion as the one I gave him from my garden."

"This year, then, is your year alone, my son. God go with you!" said his mother.

Juan took his basket, went down the four ladderlike steps from his house, shooed the ducks and chickens out of his way, and went out to the road to the village.

The hour was early, but the road was crowded with creaking carts drawn by fat, lazy *carabaos*.

Juan whistled a merry Tagalog tune as his feet danced along the road. The feast of the patron saint was the greatest celebration of the year in every village. There was music, dancing, and feasting, with prizes for this and prizes for that. From vegetable-laden carts men called to Juan, offering a ride, but he preferred to walk.

As he came within sight of the village, Juan could see the paper-flowered arches raised for the fiesta.

The ancient adobe church of San Isidro was on the edge of the village, and next to it the home of Padre Ignacio, the old Spanish priest. Padre Ignacio was Juan's very good friend.

Aie, it was a good day! But just at the corner of the Padre's land, the village bully, Pedro, darted out from behind a clump of banana trees. In the wink of an eye he tripped Juan, sending him spinning to the ground. The onions flew in every direction, their crackly skins ruined, their juice mingling with the dust of the road.

Unnoticed by either Juan or Pedro, the old priest had been watching. He was angry.

"Many a time I have warned you, Pedro," he said. "Now see what your cruelty has accomplished! Come, Juan, we must think of the exhibit."

"It is all over," said Juan. "I have nothing to exhibit. If only I had taken a ride on the cart when it was offered!"

"One does not spend time regretting; one thinks of the future," said the Padre. "Now, there is the onion you gave me from your garden, Juan, when you gave the seed to me. I have it in my house. It was so beautiful I could not cut into it, though I hungered for it, I tell you."

"You should have eaten it then, Padre," said Juan, "for there must be several vegetables to enter for the prize. One alone will never win."

"Well, son, I must hurry on. I have some business I must attend to."

All day long the gaily dressed people went up and down the streets of the small village, singing, dancing, shouting. They passed up and down the aisles of the exhibition hall where the beautiful products of their patient hands were to be seen.

But Juan did not go near the hall. His heart was too heavy. He was sitting outside the old church when Maria Flores went by, waving the ribbon she had won.

"Padre Ignacio is looking for you. He asked me to find you. I almost forgot, I was so excited about my prize. There he comes now. *Aie,* he is laughing about something. He is pleased."

"There you are, Juan," said the old priest. "Ah, but I have good news for you. You have won! Not one peso, Juan; not two pesos; not three, but five pesos you have won!"

"It is not like you to tease, Padre! I could not possibly win. I entered nothing."

"But I did it for you. I took the bowl of seed you gave me. I entered it with the beautiful onion you gave me to show what could be grown from the seed.

"And hear this, Juan. You not only won the prize of five pesos, the largest prize given, but you also won a letter of praise from the judges because you have contributed to the future of the farmers on the Bay. They will now raise onions, and only because you have shown them what can be grown from such tiny seeds with such great patience. You see, Juan, hard work is rewarded!"

Girma's Special Achievement

By Noel Habte-Mariam

Girma gulped the last of his dinner while his Aunt Etenesh watched disapprovingly. "You eat too fast, Girma," she scolded.

Girma tore a bite-sized piece of *ingera,* a soft, pancakelike Ethiopian bread, rolled it neatly around some spicy bean stew, and popped it into his mouth.

"I can't help it," he mumbled, swallowing hard. "I'm really in a hurry tonight." Then, bidding a pleasant evening, he grabbed *Mathematics for Sixth Grade* from a small stack of books near his cot and raced out the door.

It was dusk in the city of Gondar, capital of the province of Begemdir, Ethiopia. Girma had lived here for almost a year, ever since he had left the tiny village of Chilga where he had been born. When Aunt Etenesh had invited him to live with her, his father had agreed to let Girma go because he believed the schools in the provincial capital would be better than those in the countryside. But it was a hardship for Girma's father to work the farm without his son's help. Now it was up to Girma to make the sacrifice worthwhile.

Within a week, Girma and all the other sixth graders in Ethiopia would be taking an examination to determine who could go on to seventh grade. Most would pass, but not all. Although Girma had done well in school so far, he took nothing for granted. He did not want to disappoint his father.

Girma ran down winding dirt paths, past tin-roofed huts. He could see the Ethiopian tricolored flag being lowered at the center of town. Soon the streetlights will be lit, he thought. He began to walk more quickly.

Like many of the people who lived in the mountains surrounding Gondar, Girma's aunt could not afford electricity. So on many evenings, Girma and other children would head for the main road to study beneath the streetlights for an hour or two.

Tonight, Girma was in a particular hurry. He had seen workers replacing a light bulb in one of the streetlamps that afternoon, and he knew it would now be the brightest light in town. There, he hoped to find a good place to sit.

The new light came on just as Girma arrived. Several children were already studying. Girma sat down among them, and they chatted briefly. Then each became absorbed in his and her own school-work. As darkness fell, more students crowded within the circle of light. Soon the mountains were black. The distant howl of hyenas pierced the cool stillness of the night. Girma gathered his heavy cotton *gabi* around him and concentrated on his math problems. Finally, he closed his book and looked around.

Although the heaviness of his eyelids told him it must be very late, a number of students remained. Some were older students, preparing for high school examinations. Some were Girma's friends. Their serious faces were buried in well-worn books, and Girma knew how hard they were studying. There was so little time left.

Girma rose quietly and began the long walk home, his tired brain mulling over the day's events. This day he had done after-school errands for one of the high school teachers and had earned enough money to pay for some paper and pencils. He had done work for this teacher before, so this time she gave him something extra, a candy treat. Taking it out of his pocket, Girma was glad he had saved it for now. A sweet ending, he thought, to a long, hard day.

The examination day finally arrived, and a week later the results were announced. That morning Girma joined a crowd of babbling students at the school bulletin board. His eyes passed quickly over the alphabetical lists of names posted. He could not see his name! "It cannot be!" he gasped. He read the lists again. Then he noticed a separate column. "Students Honored for Special Achievement," the heading read. There was Girma's name, the only sixth-grader listed.

Feeling the glow of success, Girma read the lists a third time, looking for the names of his friends. They had all passed! His happiness was complete.

The next day Girma left his aunt's home and returned to Chilga. He was eager to make the trip before the rainy season began. There were no roads to Chilga, only dirt paths running through the rugged mountains, winding along the riverbeds and passing through tiny villages.

With the coming of the rains, the ground would be soft, rivers would overflow, and the hillsides would soon be covered with tall, thick grass. Even in good weather, Girma had to walk for three days, spending nights and sharing meals with generous farmers along the way.

When Girma arrived home, his mother and two younger sisters were working outside their *tukul,* a round, mud-walled, thatch-roofed house. They were drying colorful piles of herbs and spices in the sun. Girma's father was leading two oxen back from the fields.

"Eh, my little scholar!" Girma's mother cried when she saw him. They embraced and kissed each other several times on each cheek. Then Girma did the same with his father and sisters. "How are you? Are you fine?" they asked him over and over.

Girma told them his good news and answered their questions about Aunt Etenesh. Then, over a cup of sweet tea, they listened to Girma's description of Gondar, his teachers, and his friends.

Girma's father beamed. "So you were the only sixth-grader to earn a special achievement," he said.

"Yes," Girma admitted with pride, but he was proud of his friends, too. Many of them had spent long evenings with him, studying beneath the streetlights. He knew that they had worked as hard as he. Being good students, he felt, was a special achievement for them all.

Astradehojas Finds a Job

By Sophia Karageorges

Astradehojas is his name, and this is quite a long name for such a short, chubby man.

He is neither young nor is he old. In fact, no one in the little Greek village by the sea could say exactly how old he really is, nor how young.

Every day Astradehojas wanders through the village and smiles at everyone. Everyone smiles back at him, for everyone likes Astradehojas.

It is always warm and sunny by the sea. And every day Astradehojas wears the same brown trousers and red plaid shirt—except on Sundays he wears a blue shirt, the color of the sky and sea and his eyes. And always on top of his head is a faded, green, wide-brimmed hat, so no one can say what color his hair is, or if he has any at all.

Now, early one morning Astradehojas wandered about the village. He smiled and bowed to the women drawing water from the well. He waved and smiled at Petros, the shepherd, who was herding his flock of sheep through the village toward the green pastures near the seashore.

"Everyone is busy working," he thought. "I must find work." Then he had an idea and hurried down the village street until he came to a little shop.

"Good morning, my friend Tasio," he greeted the village shoemaker. "Let me help you make shoes."

"Good morning, Astradehojas," Tasio smiled. "Now you know you tried once to help me. You cut the pattern wrong and spoiled the leather. No, I am sorry, but I cannot let you help me."

Astradehojas continued his walk through the village and came to the baker's shop.

"Good morning, Costa, my friend. My, it smells so good in your shop! I would like to help you bake the bread today."

Costa smiled at Astradehojas but shook his head. "No, no, sorry. Remember last week you helped me and forgot the time and let the bread get too brown? No, my friend, please do not ask to help me."

Astradehojas walked away. His shoulders drooped and his smile disappeared. "Oh dear," he thought, "I must be good for something." Then his smile reappeared. "I'll go see Pavlos who owns the olive oil shop. He will let me help him."

But even Pavlos shook his head. He gave Astradehojas a friendly pat on the shoulder and said, "I am still scrubbing the floor where you spilled the big can of olive oil last week when I let you help. Why don't you go to the seashore? The boys and girls are having races and games there. Maybe they will let you judge the contests."

Astradehojas's short legs trotted fast to the seashore. He loved the children. He would be happy to judge their contests.

The children saw him coming. They smiled and waved, for they liked the little smiling man. "Hello, Astradehojas. How are you, Astradehojas?"

"Ah, you have a fine day for the contests. I have come to help. I shall be the judge."

Tike, the oldest boy, stepped forward. "I am sorry, Astradehojas. I am going to be the judge. The last time we let you be the judge, you couldn't make up your mind who was the winner."

"That is true, Tike. But I like each of you the same, so it was very difficult to decide."

"Well," said Tike, "you'd better find a nice spot to sit and watch."

So Astradehojas sat down under a tall cypress tree and watched the children's races and jumping contests. He clapped his hands for all of them, whether they were winners or losers.

The last contest was the swimming race for the boys. They lined up along the beach. Tike held his hand high.

"When I lower my arm and shout 'Go!' jump into the sea and swim to that big rock, touch it, and then turn and swim to shore. The first one to touch dry sand is the winner."

Astradehojas left the shade of the cypress tree and came to the water's edge to watch. Tike gave the command, "Go!" and the boys jumped into the sea.

"Come on!" Astradehojas shouted encouragingly.

The boys had all touched the rock and were heading back to shore. "Come on! Hurry!" Astradehojas yelled. "Come—" His voice died in his throat, for he had seen a dark shadow near the big rock. "Shark!" he screamed.

Tike saw it, too, and yelled to the boys to hurry. The dark fin of the shark cut the water behind the thrashing feet of the swimmers.

"What shall we do, Astradehojas?" Tike shrieked.

But Astradehojas was no longer on the beach. He had grabbed the pole the boys used in the vaulting contest and leaped into the sea. He had the pole between his teeth. He swam fast and passed the boys who were hurrying to reach the safety of the beach.

Then Astradehojas took the pole and beat the water. He swam and thrashed about, yelling all the while, and the sea foamed about him.

By this time all the boys were safe on shore.

"Astradehojas is frightening the shark away!" they all shouted. "Bravo, Astradehojas!"

The shark was frightened by the commotion Astradehojas had stirred up, and headed out to sea.

Word of Astradehojas's bravery spread swiftly through the village. Everyone gathered around him and shook his hand and patted him on the back. "Bravo, Astradehojas!"

Finally Pavlos stepped forward and held up his hands for silence. "Listen, my friends, listen! We all know how our friend Astradehojas always wants to be of help to us, but he can never find just the right job. Now I have an idea. Our children love to swim in the sea. Often no adult is with them. We have seen it can be very dangerous. I propose that we make Astradehojas the guardian of our seashore, so we will know our children will be safe while we are busy in our shops."

Now every day Astradehojas can be found at the seashore with the children. The village carpenter has built him a high platform, and there he sits and watches over the children—smiling all the while.

Ntombi of Swaziland

By James A. Jones

"Uunngh! I hate to get up." Ntombi rubbed her eyes. From across the room, snores proved that her brother was still asleep. Outside, the sky was growing light, and the roosters were beginning to crow. Her older brother was lucky; he could sleep late.

Ntombi dressed quietly and stepped outside. In the dim light she could see the other small buildings of her family's *kraal*. Beyond them was the cow pen she was headed for. She found the bucket in the cooking building, where her mother was already making a fire. Down to the pen to milk the cows—that was how she started every day.

After finishing, she chased the cows uphill to the pasture and went back to the cooking building. It was smoky and warm inside. Ntombi sat by the fire next to her father and brother. To take away the damp chill of the mountain morning, her mother gave her a cup of sweet tea mixed with milk. The weather is mostly warm in Swaziland, but sometimes at night, fog forms in the valleys. "Hot tea is a good way to warm up in the early morning," her mother said.

Soon it was time for Ntombi, her brother, Maphewa, and her little sister, Sala, to start walking to school. The path followed the valley to a river. On the other side they came to the road to Hlatikulu, the nearest town. There were many people on the road, going to school or to the market in town.

They walked through the school gate just as the bell rang. Ntombi stood in line with her class while the headmaster made announcements and passed out the mail. There are no mailboxes in Swaziland; letters are often sent to schools and carried home by the students. After mail call everyone sang the national anthem before going to class.

Ntombi is in Form One, which is like eighth grade. Her morning classes were the hardest: science, English, and mathematics. She spoke English very well, but it was hard to write without making any mistakes.

The afternoon was easier. First there was history. That afternoon her teacher talked about how Swaziland stayed independent of its big neighbors, South Africa and Mozambique. Her last class was Zulu. That was almost like Ntombi's language, Siswati, so it was not too hard for her. The class read a story about the great Shaka, who united the Zulu people into one nation.

When classes ended at three o'clock, all of the children gathered to play soccer in the school yard. Ntombi liked to play with her friends. They played with a leather ball in the grassy yard until the sun started to turn gold in the west. If they wanted to find the cows before dark, it was time to go home.

Ntombi and her brother and sister walked together. Just before they reached the *kraal,* Maphewa said to Sala, "Will you take my books? I see the cows."

Both older children gave their books to Sala and raced up the hill. When they got near the cows, Ntombi pretended to be one of Shaka's warriors, stalking through the grass. The cows knew this game. They could eat until the warriors attacked, then they would have to go back home.

By the time the gate was closed, dinner was ready in their father's building. Father gave thanks for their food: chicken stew, mealy-meal (a kind of cornmeal) porridge, and more tea. Tea and porridge were normal, but the chicken was a treat.

After dinner Ntombi and Maphewa started toward their building. There was no moon, and the stars looked like sparks from a giant white sparkler. They waited to see who could spot the first shooting star. After a few minutes, Ntombi shouted, "There's one!" Her father heard her and came out.

"Don't you have homework to do? Go do it. You will have to go to sleep soon."

The two children went inside and lit a candle. They were finished studying when their father came back to say good night.

Under the covers Ntombi imagined the whole sky full of shooting stars. They faded slowly as she fell asleep.

The Dragon's Bristle

By D.J. Chaconas

Pieter ran through the pink-white orchard, then over the small stone bridge of the canal. Jan's house was just ahead—white with an orange roof, like the other Belgian farmhouses.

"Jan," he called, "are you ready? We will be leaving soon for Mons. The festival is waiting."

"Come in, Pieter," Jan's mother said from the kitchen window. "Jan is in his room."

Filled with excitement, Pieter ran to him. "Today we will chase the dragon and pull a bristle from its tail. And with the good luck the bristles will bring, we will wish for the bicycles!" He jerked to a stop at the sight of Jan's long face. Jan was sitting in bed, bundled up in blankets.

"I'm sick," Jan said, his voice almost quivering. "I can't go to the festival with you."

"Not go? But you will miss St. George and your chance at the dragon's tail. You won't be able to wish for your bicycle."

"I know," Jan murmured. "And I've waited so long for this day."

"Oh, Jan—"

"You had better hurry, Pieter. Your family will be leaving."

"Are you sure you can't come?"

Jan nodded. "It's just a cold, but I must stay in bed. Will you come later to tell me about it?"

"I'll come," Pieter promised, then left and ran for home.

As the family car made its way to Mons, Pieter dreamed of the dragon. "I will have to be fast," he thought, "for the dragon will be protected by the wild men with their leather balloons. They will beat off anyone who comes near."

He thought of his wish, closing his eyes to picture the shiny new bicycle. But all he could see was Jan's sad face.

74

I wish he could have come, Pieter thought, remembering the plans they had made together.

Reaching Mons, they drove to the heart of the festival, the Grande Place. Pieter's spirits sank even further when he saw the town square filled with hundreds of people. He knew they were all waiting for St. George and a chance at getting a bristle from the dragon's tail.

"I probably won't even get a bristle," he said to himself, walking through the crowd, looking for a spot from which the dragon was likely to come. "There are so many people."

The bells started to chime. Pieter listened to the beautiful tones, casually at first, and then he listened more closely. That was strange. The bells seemed to call to him, "Here, Pieter, here." Listening, he followed the ringing through the crowded Grande Place to the bell tower.

As soon as he reached it, the people started to send up a confusion of cries. "It's the dragon!" Pieter felt the back of his head tingle. He slowly lifted his eyes—up and up and up. The giant green head of the dragon swayed high above him, like a menacing cloud. His heart jumped at the sight of it, and he caught his breath. The bells had called him! The dragon was entering the square from behind the bell tower.

The dragon lumbered out, and the people rushed for its tail with Pieter leading them.

"The wild men!" someone cried. "Watch out for the wild men!" The crowd screamed and laughed, hurrying back to safety. But Pieter would not be frightened by their threatening noises and harmless leather balloons. He dove for the dragon's tail while the wild men jumped and screeched and beat him. The crowd charged in again.

Pieter bent his head, ducking what blows he could, his hands searching for a bristle. They searched over the heavy cloth tail, and "Ouch!" they slid into something stiff and sharp. A bristle! He pulled—hard! The bristle popped out.

Clutching it, Pieter started to wish. With his eyes closed, he didn't see the wild man strike out. Like a shock, he felt the leather balloon land firmly on his hand. His eyes flashed open but too late. The prized bristle was gone!

"No! Oh, no!" Pieter cried to the crowd. "I had a bristle. I was wishing. Now it's lost!" But the crowd didn't hear him. They were already chasing the dragon to the far side of the square.

Slowly and sadly Pieter went to join his family for the rest of the day. He tried to be as cheerful as they were, but his mind kept returning to the lost bristle and the lost wish.

The ride home seemed too long for Pieter. He was eager to see Jan. Almost as soon as the car stopped, he was hurrying across the fields to tell his friend about the bristle.

When he reached his friend's house, Jan sat up in bed, "Did you get a bristle?" he asked, his eyebrows popping up like question marks.

"I—I had one. But I lost it."

"Lost it! Oh, Pieter! I'm sorry."

Both boys sighed, sitting back in silence, not knowing what to say about such a terrible loss. Their eyes studied the rugs on the floor. Jan's eyes came to Pieter's dusty shoes. He looked away, then quickly looked back again. There was something sticking out from Pieter's shoe.

"What's that?" Jan asked, pointing.

Pieter leaned over for a look, then lifted his face to look at Jan. His eyes were opened wide in amazement.

"The bristle! The lost bristle! It must have fallen into my shoe!"

Jan started to bounce on the bed. "Now you can wish," he said excitedly. "Oh, Pieter, you are so lucky!"

"You mean WE are lucky," Pieter said without even thinking. "After all, you found the bristle, too. It belongs to both of us."

Then Pieter held one end of the bristle and offered the other end to Jan. He accepted it, a warm smile of friendship glowing from his face. Together they closed their eyes to wish, and for one whole minute, the room was very—very—quiet.

A Gypsy Fortune

By S. Jones Rogan

The sun warmed Myrtle's skin as she breathed in the sweet scent of the hedgerows. She loved this time of year—summer's end and time for school to begin.

"Steady there, Peg," Myrtle commanded the gray pony that was harnessed to the Gypsy wagon. "How's the wheel, Papa?"

"Holding up so far, lass. We'll have to take it slow and steady, mind. But the wheelwright in

Bryncrug should be able to fix it." He ran his hand along the split in the rear wheel.

The pony chomped on her bit. "Don't worry, Peg. You'll get your hay and your oats soon enough," Myrtle said, laughing. Peg was her best friend in all of Wales. Myrtle had even chosen Peg's name. Peg was dependable and strong, like the wooden pegs her father carved and sold. What with mending pots and pans and telling fortunes, they made a tinker's living.

Myrtle opened a battered book and added up their earnings. "Almost five pounds, Papa, including last week." She watched her father's face, dark like rich leather, crease into a frown. He pulled at his gold earring.

"Not enough for fixing that wheel and for school books. I'm sorry, Myrtle, you won't be able to go to school for a while. . . . What's that noise?"

A strange wailing sound became louder as it approached them. Suddenly, a motorbike appeared from around a bend. Astride it was a man wearing a leather cap and round goggles, his coattails flapping in the wind.

The motorbike roared like an angry dragon, and coughed filthy black smoke. Myrtle stuck her fingers in her ears. The bike zoomed past and then backfired. *Crack!*

Startled, Peg reared onto her stocky hind legs, hurling Myrtle backward into the caravan. The pony bolted, eyes wide in a frenzy. She galloped madly along the winding Welsh road. The caravan lurched from side to side. Their heavy cooking cauldron, carried underneath the wagon, was torn loose and bounced into the air.

With all her strength, Myrtle heaved herself forward. But each time Peg rounded another bend, she was thrown back. It's no good, she thought frantically. I'm not strong enough. Myrtle tried one more time.

Inch by inch, she managed to climb onto the bench and grab the reins. She pulled them in with all her might. "Please, oh please, Peg, stop!" she cried to the frightened pony.

As though realizing that her young friend was terrified, Peg slowed down. Too late. The sound of splintering wood echoed in Myrtle's ears, and the rear wheel collapsed. Peg was dragged down by the weight of the skidding wagon, her legs buckling beneath her. She lay still.

Myrtle, bruised and shaken, dropped the reins and rushed to Peg's side. "You're safe now," she soothed. Myrtle tried to undo the harness, but it was caught under the broken wagon. "Where's Papa?" she sobbed.

Turning at the sound of the approaching motor-bike, Myrtle sighed with relief, for sitting behind the man was her father.

"I'm most awfully sorry. The bike backfired accidentally," said the man, pulling off his goggles.

"Thank goodness you're all right, lass." Myrtle's father ran to her.

"Papa, Peg can't move," she sobbed. "She's caught up something terrible." Myrtle glared at the stranger.

Her father looked at the tangle of reins and harness. Peg's back leg was jutting out in a grotesque manner. "We'll have to jack up the cart and cut her free. If she starts to struggle, she'll break that leg for sure."

Myrtle's stomach churned. If Peg were badly injured, she would have to be put out of her misery. Hot tears streamed down Myrtle's cheeks. "Papa, you and *gaje* lift the cart. I'll go underneath to cut the harness."

"Nay, lass. It's too dangerous. If Peg made a single move, the wagon would fall on top of you."

"Please, Papa. She'll hold still if I tell her to," Myrtle pleaded.

Reluctantly, her father agreed. There was no other choice. He handed Myrtle the sharp knife he used for woodcarving.

"Heave!" he grunted, as the men leaned on an old fence post they'd wedged under the heavy wagon. Slowly, it rose off the ground.

Myrtle scrambled underneath, the hard road scraping her bare knees. She cut the harness.

The pony tossed her head. The caravan began to slip.

"Be still, Peg. You're nearly free," said Myrtle in a firm voice. The wagon creaked above her head. Ignoring her fear, Myrtle cut through the mess of leather strapping. The pony lay still.

"There!" Myrtle made the final cut and scampered out from beneath the wagon. Her father now unharnessed Peg with ease. The pony whinnied and clambered to her feet.

"Oh, Papa!" breathed Myrtle. "She's standing."

"Aye, lass. Thanks to you."

The stranger reached inside his coat. "Look, I'm terribly sorry about all this, but I really must leave. I hope this covers the damage," he said, thrusting money into Myrtle's hand. Then, in a cloud of smoke, he was gone.

With her velvety nose, Peg nudged Myrtle, who was counting the money. "Papa! There's fifty pounds here!" Myrtle exclaimed.

"Well, what do you know?" he said. "It's a Gypsy's fortune." He surveyed the ruins of their caravan and belongings. "We have to fix all this and get you off to Bryncrug, before school starts tomorrow." He winked at Myrtle.

Myrtle patted the pony's neck and smiled. How she loved this time of year.

PANCHO'S FERRY

By Bill Bollinger

Pancho glanced hopefully toward the road, but there were no cars waiting to be ferried across the river. For more than a week now there had been no cars—not since the bridge was finished.

"Why did they do this to us, Grandfather?" Pancho asked suddenly. "Why did they build the bridge?"

Antonio Martinez lowered his pipe and turned slowly to face Pancho. The rough wooden barge on which they were sitting bobbed slowly in the river's current, tugging gently at the thick ropes that held it moored beneath the overhanging trees.

"Progress, Pancho," he answered at last. "The bridge will make it easier for the tourists to reach the high mountains."

"But since they built the bridge, not one car has come down the steep banks of the canyon to ride our ferryboat," Pancho cried. "How will we live?"

Quietly the old man tapped his pipe against the railing and then slowly put it away. "We'll have to leave our river, Pancho," he said sadly. "Perhaps one of the sheep ranches will hire me. I was a shepherd long before I was a ferryman."

Pancho stood up abruptly. "No, Grandfather. Our home is here. I'll go up to the bridge and try to persuade some of the tourists to ride our ferry across the river."

He leaped from the barge and marched up the steep, winding road. He didn't stop until he was near the gleaming new tollhouse that stood at the beginning of the bridge. Several cars were waiting their turn to cross the bridge. Far down the road, almost hidden by the line of honking cars, an old shepherd with a few scraggly sheep was slowly plodding toward the bridge.

"I wonder what the toll will be for a sheep!" Pancho laughed. But he quickly forgot the old man and his sheep when he remembered why he had come to the bridge.

Pancho approached a car and spoke up bravely. "Say, Mister, would you like to be ferried across the river? It's only a quarter, no more than the toll."

"No, I'm sorry," the man answered. "The bridge is much faster."

Pancho started to tug at his arm, then dropped his half-raised hand. Maybe the next one. But the next one didn't want to ride the ferry either. Or the one after that. Or the next.

Disappointed, Pancho shoved his hands deep into the pockets of his jeans and walked back to the tollhouse to wait for another carload of tourists. He noticed several roughly dressed men sitting on the curb, watching the cars.

Sheep ranchers, Pancho thought. I'll go over there and sit with them.

He found a seat on the curb by a slender man with crinkly blue eyes. The man winked at him and then turned back to the other ranchers and began to talk intently. They all seemed to be worried about something.

Pancho had seen most of the men before. They used to drive their huge herds of sheep across the ford just below the ferry. The water was shallow there, and the sheep could cross the river easily.

"Well, the bridge has fixed that, too," Pancho whispered. "They built it right on top of the ford.

Now the ranchers will have to go many miles downriver to get their sheep across."

Suddenly a hush fell over the crowd. Even the ranchers interrupted their conversation to see what was happening. The old shepherd had reached the tollhouse, and his sheep were milling about, bleating mournfully.

"But I've got to cross your bridge," he was complaining loudly. "I have to. If I go by the ford downriver, it will take me another day. If I don't hurry, someone else will get the pasture in the mountains that I've been using all these years!"

The tollhouse keeper's face reddened, and he shoved his cap back with one hand and braced the other on his hip. "You don't understand," he said. "The bridge was built for cars, not sheep. If you were to take your sheep across, we would have to stop traffic until you reached the other side. We can't do that."

The old man's shoulders slumped. "Just this once?" he pleaded.

"No, I'm sorry," the keeper said. "We don't do it for others, and we must treat everyone the same."

Wearily the shepherd turned from the bridge.

"Another one with trouble," Pancho said. "Maybe I can help him. I'm sure Grandfather won't mind ferrying sheep across the river just this once!"

Pancho yelled loudly so that his voice would carry to the shepherd, "I'll help you across!" To his surprise everyone turned to look at him. "I'll help you across," he repeated, more meekly this time.

The shepherd stared at him. "How can you help me?" he asked.

"The ferry," Pancho replied. "My grandfather owns the ferry. We can ferry your sheep across the river."

"What did you say, boy? Say that again!" a rough voice barked suddenly near Pancho's shoulder. It was the rancher who had winked at him earlier that day.

"I told him we would ferry his sheep across the river," Pancho repeated. "Otherwise he will have to go many miles out of his way."

The rancher turned suddenly and motioned for the other men to come closer. "Did you hear that?" he questioned. "Now why didn't we think of that? The boy's going to take the sheep over on his grandfather's barge."

He turned back to Pancho. "I want to be next," he declared. "I'll pay you well. Ferrying the sheep across here will save my hauling them by truck to the lower ford. Whatever you charge will cost less than that. I can drive them to pasture just as I always did, and—"

The rancher's voice was drowned out by others clamoring for Pancho's attention, making arrangements for their sheep to be ferried over the river.

"Come, follow me!" Pancho exclaimed. "Come talk to my grandfather. He's the ferryman." Pancho turned and scrambled rapidly down the steep bank. His grandfather wouldn't have to worry about work now. There would be more business than ever before. They might even have to build another barge for all those sheep!

"Grandfather," Pancho called. "Grandfather, I have good news."

The Klompen Maker

By Ann Lenssen

The arms of the windmill cast long shadows on the wall of the shop. Enough for today, thought the old shoemaker. He carefully covered the wood blocks to keep them from drying out.

Just then his wife appeared from the back rooms that served as their living quarters. "How did you do?" she asked.

"Today I made only two pairs of klompen," he sighed heavily, rubbing his aching shoulders. "Mrs. Van Zee will have to wait another day for her new shoes. I do not work as quickly as I used to, you know."

"Tomorrow will be better. You'll see," she comforted. "Come. Have some hot tea and bread."

Early the next day, the old man was back at work in his shop. He peeled layers of wood from willow blocks until they were just the right shape. Then he carved out the openings, bit by bit. The pile of wood curls on the floor grew deeper.

"May I watch you work?"

Startled, the old man looked up. Before him stood a ragged boy, about twelve years old. "Who are you?" he asked. "How long have you been standing here?"

"The tools must be very sharp to cut the wood that way," said the boy, ignoring the shoemaker's questions. "My father once said that knowing how to carve a piece of wood into something useful is a gift."

"Your father is a wise man," answered the shoemaker. "Why are you not at home with him?"

The boy looked down quickly. "I have no father. Not since the sea came through the dike."

"That is most unfortunate. Then your mother must need you even more."

The boy shook his head. "There is no one." He took a deep breath. "My name is Hendrik, and I am looking for work. I can sweep floors and sharpen your tools."

The old man hesitated. The lad's clothing was torn and soiled, and a tattered woolen cap covered his head. The boy pulled his rumpled coat closer, shivering.

"You need a job," agreed the shoemaker. "But I am very poor. I could not pay you even a guilder in a month."

"Let me try for one week," the boy pleaded. "Could I have meals instead? And a place to sleep?"

The old man nodded. "That is a fair bargain. Now come inside. My wife will bring you some food. Here. Put your coat and hat on this rack."

Hendrik hung up his coat, but pulled his cap down over his ears. "My head gets cold easily."

"Indeed?" the shoemaker gave the boy a curious look, then turned to his worktable. While the old man carved, Hendrik swept up piles of wood curls and restored the cutting edge of each blade.

"Three pairs today," said the shoemaker that night to his wife. "Hendrik is a good helper. Tomorrow I will show him how to use the tools he sharpened so well."

The next day Hendrik listened as the shoemaker instructed him. "Always keep the wood damp, or it may split open when you work with it. No one wants klompen with cracks where the water leaks in! Now you try. Press the tool into the wood and turn it. Be careful . . . there. That's right. And again. Very good!"

Hendrik's thin hands were strong and sure. The tools did not slip in his grasp.

"You are a natural," exclaimed the old man. "Have you worked with wood before?"

"Only the wooden ducks I used to carve. See? I still have one in my pocket." He gave it to the shoemaker, who studied its delicate wings and satiny finish.

"This is astonishing work for a lad your age, Hendrik. You have remarkable ability."

That night after dinner, the shoemaker spoke earnestly to Hendrik. "You will be a man soon, and klompen making is a man's job. You could take my place in the shop. I have spoken of this to my wife, and she agrees." The old woman nodded.

Hendrik's lip quivered, and he looked at the floor. He stuffed his hands in his pockets. "I'm not sure. It's just that . . ." He hesitated.

"What is it?" asked the old man.

"We thought you liked the work," said his wife.

"I do! But you s-s-see . . . ," stammered Hendrik, rubbing his forehead. His face was sad as he gazed at the old man and woman. Suddenly, he pulled off his woolen cap. Long blond hair tumbled down.

"Hendrik, you are a girl!" gasped the old man, his face paling. "But why didn't you tell us?"

"I had to disguise myself," she said. "I was alone. It was easier for a boy to find work. I suppose you will not want me to stay now." She stuffed her hair back under the cap. "My name is really Dena. I will go. Thank you for all you have done." She slipped out the door and started to walk down the path.

"No, wait!" the old woman called after her. "We need you!"

Dena stopped and turned.

But the shoemaker shook his head. "A girl klompen maker? That's unheard of! The village will laugh, and no one will come to the shop."

"She's good with the tools," reminded his wife.

"I would like to stay. We'd be a family," said Dena wistfully.

"Folks will say I've been knocked silly by the arms of the windmill," said the shoemaker.

"They'll change their minds in time," reassured his wife.

The old man looked at Dena's hopeful expression. He relented. "You belong here," he told her. "Please remain with us."

And so she did. Before long, people came great distances to watch the only girl klompen maker they'd ever heard of. The shoes Dena made were beautiful, and each person who bought a pair discovered a wonderful thing. Tucked in the toe of one shoe was a special gift—a tiny, delicately carved duck.